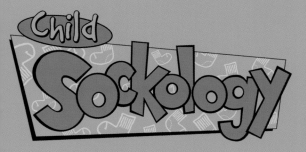

To Cheese
or Not To Cheese
The Story of Ruth

Written and Illustrated by
Damon J. Taylor

KREGEL
Kidzone

FOR PARENTS
with Dr. Sock

This story will help children understand the importance of being selfless and thinking of others when making decisions.

Read It Together–

The story of Ruth and Naomi is found in the Old Testament book of Ruth.

Sharing–

Discuss with your child a time from your childhood when you were selfish, or a time when you made a decision that was selfless and considerate.

Discussion Starters–

• Would you be an Orpah or a Ruth?

• How can we be more selfless?

• Do you think there was a time when Ruth thought about leaving Naomi?

• Are there any widows or elderly people who we as a family could care for?

For Fun–

Visit a home for the elderly or elderly people from church. Ask them questions. Are they from another country? Do they have family nearby?

Draw–

Draw with your kids. Have them draw pictures of themselves with their grandparents or with other older family members.

Prayer Time–

After reading the story, pray with your kids. Thank God for being at the center of your lives. Ask God to place someone in your midst who might benefit from your family's friendship.

COLEMAN HAS FOUND THAT THE LIFE OF A LITTLE BOY

can be tough at times, especially if that boy has a baby sister named Shelby. When Shelby was born, Coleman needed a way to deal with his day-to-day problems. He found his socks. Yes, that's right, his socks.

It may seem weird, but these aren't your regular, everyday tube socks that you find in your dresser. As ordinary as they may appear, these socks really are Coleman's friends, and they help him with his problems. When life gets complicated, Coleman goes to his bedroom and works through his troubles by playing make-believe with his socks and remembering Bible stories he's learned.

So please sit back, take off your shoes and socks if you like, and enjoy Coleman's imaginary world in . . .

To Cheese or Not to Cheese
The Story of Ruth

To Great-Grandma Ruth Deckard
(92 and living large)

Coleman is sitting alone in his bedroom. He is thinking, thinking hard. Earlier, Coleman's mom asked him to get dressed for Great-Grandma Ruth's ninety-second birthday dinner.

This explains why he's in his room, but it doesn't explain why he's sitting and thinking instead of getting dressed.

AM I THINKING HARD OR JUST REGULAR THINKING, OR AM I THINKING ABOUT HOW I'M THINKING?

He's sitting
and thinking because his friend Andrew invited
Coleman to go with him and his family to eat at
Stinky Cheese's, "Home of the Limburger Cheese
Pizza and Skeeball-o-rama."

Coleman would rather go to Stinky's and have
a good time than sit at some boring dinner for his
Great-Grandma Ruth, and he was bold enough to
say so to his mom.

That's why he's now in his room, thinking. Mom sent him there to think about his selfish attitude and how it should change before dinnertime.

"Hi Coleman. What's bugging you?" asked Sockariah, one of Coleman's imaginary sock buddies.

"I'm supposed to sit here and think about my selfish attitude," Coleman answered. "I don't want to go to Great-Grandma Ruth's birthday dinner."

"Can I help you think?" asked Sockariah. "I remember a story from the Bible that might help. It's about another woman named Ruth."

"It happened a long time ago, at a time when the people of Israel didn't have enough to eat. . . ."

Elimelech and his wife, Naomi, had two sons. They moved from Bethlehem to Moab in hopes of finding a better life. For Elimelech, this wasn't meant to be.

He died. The two boys grew up and married two Moabite women named Orpah and Ruth.

Ten years after their weddings, both of Naomi's sons died.

"Sockariah, this story isn't making me think about changing my mind, it's making me nervous about ever getting married," said Coleman as he squirmed uncomfortably on his bed.

"Just sit still and listen, Cole."

Naomi, Orpah, and Ruth were now alone. Naomi told Orpah and Ruth to go back to their families and start their lives over. They were young and pretty, and they had their whole lives still ahead of them.

Orpah took Naomi's advice. She packed up her things and went home. Ruth did not.

Ruth could have left Naomi alone in a strange land with no one to take care of her, but she didn't.

Ruth told Naomi, "I want to stay with you. You are my family now. And the God of your people is now my God, too. I will stay with you to the end."

This pleased Naomi, and although they didn't know it at the time, Ruth's loyalty pleased God, too.

Bethlehem

Naomi heard that there was now food in her homeland. So she and Ruth went to live in Bethlehem.

Back in those days, widows and older people had a hard time earning a living. But Naomi and Ruth were determined to take care of themselves.

Naomi was old and couldn't work in the grain fields, so Ruth did the hard work.

The people of Bethlehem saw this young Moabite woman taking good care of her mother-in-law. They spoke well of Ruth.

One day, while Ruth gathered grain left behind in a field by workers, a wealthy landowner named Boaz saw her.

He asked the workers, "Who is this stranger who works so hard picking up the scraps of grain that you all leave behind?"

They told Boaz the sad story of Ruth and Naomi.

The next day, Boaz told his workers, "Let Ruth gather the grain with you so that she will get more than just leftovers." Ruth was overjoyed at Boaz's kindness.

She went home that night with plenty of food. Ruth told Naomi of Boaz's generosity, and Naomi praised God for His protection and kindness.

Boaz's kindness to
Ruth continued, and she
and Naomi always had enough grain.

The more Boaz saw of Ruth, the more he thought,
"This is an amazing woman. She is selfless and kind,
and pretty, too. I would be a blessed man to have her
as my wife."

Boaz soon asked Ruth to marry him. She accepted
his proposal, and they were married.

"What happened to Naomi? Ruth got a new life, but what did Naomi get?" asked Coleman.

God blessed Ruth and Boaz with a son, and he was a special grandson to Naomi.

Naomi loved her grandson. She cared for him and spoiled him, just like your Great-Grandma Ruth spoils you.

"So Coleman, what did you learn from that story?" asked Sockariah.

"Well, I learned that Orpah missed out on a chance for a good life."

"That's true," said Sockariah. "Did you learn anything else?"

"I learned that I'll have plenty of chances to go to Stinky Cheese's, but Great-Grandma Ruth is only gonna have one ninety-second birthday, and I don't want to miss it!"

"I'm gonna go tell mom that I want to go to
Great-Gram's birthday dinner."

"Hey Sockariah, guess what! Great-Grandma Ruth told my parents that for her birthday dinner she'd like to go to Stinky Cheese's. She loves to play Skeeball-o-rama, and she thinks Stinky is the greatest."

"God is good, really good!"

The Child Sockology Series

For ages up to 5
Baby Boy, Bundle of Joy
Bible Babies
Bible Characters A to Z
Bible Numbers 1 to 10
Bible Opposites
New Testament Bible Feelings
Old Testament Bible Feelings
Times We Pray

For ages 5 and up
A Little Man with a Big Plan: The Story of Young David
The Ark and the Park: The Story of Noah
Beauty and the Booster: The Story of Esther
Forgive and Forget: The Story of Joseph
Francis Takes a Tumble: The Story of the Good Samaritan
Hide and Sink: The Story of Jonah
Lunchtime Life Change: The Story of Zacchaeus
To Cheese or Not To Cheese: The Story of Ruth